Anonymous

Death of President Brigham Young

Brief Sketch of his Life and Labors

Anonymous

Death of President Brigham Young
Brief Sketch of his Life and Labors

ISBN/EAN: 9783337096328

Printed in Europe, USA, Canada, Australia, Japan

Cover: Foto ©Raphael Reischuk / pixelio.de

More available books at **www.hansebooks.com**

OF

PRESIDENT BRIGHAM YOUNG.

BRIEF SKETCH

OF

HIS LIFE AND LABORS.

FUNERAL CEREMONIES,

WITH

FULL REPORT OF THE ADDRESSES.

RESOLUTIONS OF RESPECT, Etc.

SALT LAKE CITY, UTAH:

PRINTED AT THE DESERET NEWS STEAM PRINTING ESTABLISHMENT.

1877.

PARTICULARS

OF THE

DEATH OF PREST. BRIGHAM YOUNG

AND ACCOUNT OF

THE FUNERAL CEREMONIES.

[From the Deseret Evening News, August 29, 1877.]

DEATH OF PRESIDENT BRIGHAM YOUNG.

AT four o'clock this afternoon, PRESIDENT BRIGHAM YOUNG departed this life, surrounded by his family and intimate friends. This announcement will thrill the whole Territory with grief. We feel the weight of this great loss to the world, and cannot at this moment express in the faintest degree, our deep sense of the void occasioned by his departure. He was a GREAT MAN in every sense of the term. And he has left a mark upon the age which the future will never efface, but which will grow brighter and broader as the man, his deeds and his sentiments become better known and appreciated.

To the Latter-day Saints he has been for more than thirty-three years a counselor, a father, a friend, a guide, and a tower of strength. To all mankind he has been a prophet and a benefactor so far as they would accept his advice and receive of his teachings.

He has, under God, rescued thousands from poverty and raised them to independence, opened the deserts of these mountains to colonization, preached the gospel of salvation to many nations, declared the counsel of heaven to the inhabitants of the earth, prepared the way in the Temples of God for the redemption of hosts of the dead, organized and consolidated the order of the everlasting Priesthood, and, having finished his work on earth, gone into the spirit world to join with Joseph, Hyrum, Willard, Jedediah, Heber, George A. and other great and glorious servants of the Lord, to continue the divine work they all labored for on earth.

We mourn his departure. But they rejoice in great gain. If a mighty man has left us in grief, a mightier spirit is received among them with welcomings and gladness. For, his freed soul, no longer clogged

A

with the cares and pains of fading mortality, will wield a potent influence behind the veil.

President Brigham Young was born June 1st, 1801, at Whitingham, Windham County, Vermont. He was consequently aged 76 years, 2 months and 28 days. We have neither time nor space at this late hour to give any lengthy account of his life and career, but reserve further remarks for another occasion.

We join with the Latter-day Saints throughout the world in deep sorrow for the loss of our President, one of earth's greatest and noblest minds, but, bearing in mind that the Father of all knoweth what is best, we submit to the divine decree and say, "the will of the Lord be done."

[From the Deseret Evening News, Aug. 30, 1877.]

OBITUARY.

The tidings of the death of President Brigham Young, announced in last evening's DESERET NEWS, were telegraphed to all parts of the Union. The leading papers of the United States have each published an obituary notice, the cable has flashed the word to Europe, and all parts of the civilized world have been stirred to their depths by the sad news. The name of Brigham Young is familiar all over the globe. His greatness is universally acknowledged, but his goodness is known only to a few.

The marks of his genius are stamped on the history and travels of the Church of Jesus Christ of Latter-day Saints, on the city he loved so well, and on the towns, farms, orchards, canals, highways, railroads, telegraphs, private and public buildings, and the thousand and one witnesses to his guiding hand and counseling voice over five hundred miles of country redeemed from a desert. They have uttered his fame with a voice that has penetrated to the uttermost parts of the earth.

But his goodness, appreciation of the truth, love for that which is pure and right; detestation of vice and iniquity; desires for the welfare of the Latter-day Saints, spiritual and temporal; regard for the benefit of the whole human race, living and dead; his spirituality, refined taste, earnest faith and devotion to God; and his inspirational, prophetic, and soul-winning qualities are known but to the people who have been gathered from all parts of the earth under his administration, and fully understood and appreciated only by those who were intimately acquainted with him.

The subject of this brief sketch was born in Whitingham, Windham County, Vermont, June 1, 1801.

His father, John Young, was born March 7, 1763, in Hopkinton, Middlesex County, Massachusetts. At the age of sixteen he enlisted in the American Revolutionary Army, and served under General Washington. He was in three campaigns in his native State and in New Jersey. In 1785 he married Nabby Howe, daughter of Phinehas and Susannah Howe, who bore him five sons and six daughters. He moved to Vermont in January, 1801, and remained there three years, opening new farms.

His grandfather, Joseph Young, was a physician and surgeon in the French and Indian war, and was killed by the falling of a pole from a fence, in 1769.

His parents moved from Vermont to Sherburne, Chenango County, New York, in 1804, where, as he grew in years, he assisted in the arduous labors incident to opening farms in a heavily timbered region, enduring the privations and hardships common to forming new settlements at that period, and was restricted by circumstances to only eleven days' schooling.

At the age of sixteen, by his fathers' permission, he began engaging in business for himself. Though trained by his parents, who were Methodists, to lead a strictly moral life, he made no profession of religion until he was in his twenty-second year, when he joined that body.

October 8, 1824, he married Miriam Works, and resided in Cayuga County, New York, until the spring of 1829, following the occupation of carpenter, joiner, painter and glazier, when he moved to Mendon, Monroe County, New York. In the spring of 1830 he first saw the Book of Mormon, which was brought there by Samuel H. Smith. In the fall of 1831 Elders Alpheus Gifford, Elial Strong and others came to that place to preach the gospel as taught by Joseph Smith. He heard and believed, and after careful and prayerful reflection upon the principles revealed in the Book of Mormon, he was baptized April 14, 1832, a member of the religious organization now known as the Church of Jesus Christ of Latter-day Saints, and ordained an Elder, immediately after confirmation, Eleazer Miller officiating in each instance. Three weeks after, his wife was also baptized. During the following summer he preached the gospel in the regions adjacent to Mendon, baptizing many and organizing branches. His wife died September 8, 1832, leaving him two little girls, one two years and the other seven years of age. In the fall of 1832 he visited Kirtland, Ohio, in company with Heber C. Kimball and his brother Joseph Young and made the acquaintance of the Prophet Joseph Smith. During the evening of the day they first met, Joseph called upon Brother Brigham to pray. While doing so he spoke in tongues. The Prophet declared that he spoke in the pure Adamic language, and after he had left the room Joseph said, "The time will come when Brother Brigham Young will preside over this Church."

In company with his brother Joseph he spent a portion of the winter of 1832–3 in and around West Laboro, Canada, preaching, baptizing and organizing branches. He spent most of the spring and summer of 1833 in missionary labors in Canada and northern New York. In July he conducted a small company of Saints to Kirtland, moved his family there in the fall, and labored at his trade, preaching as opportunity offered.

In February 1833 he married Mary Ann Angel, who took charge of his children and kept house for him faithfully.

On the 5th of May, 1834, he started for Missouri, in Zion's Camp, in which he was captain of ten; arrived in Clay County on the 23d of June, returned to Kirtland in August, having performed a journey of 2000 miles on foot, and spent the remainder of the year in finishing the printing office and school room and laboring on the Temple.

He was selected one of the Quorum of the Twelve Apostles on the 14th of February, 1835. From this time till 1837, he mostly passed the winter in Kirtland, in laboring at his trade and upon the Temple, and spent the remainder of his time in traveling, holding Conferences, preaching, and regulating and organizing Branches in the East. He attended the Hebrew School at Kirtland in the winter of 1835–6, and from February 22nd to March 27th, 1836, he superintended the painting and finishing of the Temple. He attended the Solemn Assembly at the dedication and received his blessings, after which he traveled through New York, Vermont, Massachusetts and Rhode Island, attended Conference at Portland, Maine, returned to Kirtland, defended the Prophet Joseph against accusers and apostates, took a special business mission to the Eastern States, in company with Dr. Willard Richards, which he accomplished, and returned.

On the 22nd of December, 1837, he left Kirtland, on his way to Missouri, and arrived in Far West, Caldwell County, on the 14th of March, 1838. While in Missouri he purchased land and improved a handsome farm, labored diligently in the duties of his Apostleship, especially in planning for and assisting the Saints in leaving the State under the exterminating order of Governor Lilburn W. Boggs, and on the 14th of February, 1839, moved from that State with his family, leaving all his landed and nearly all his personal property. During this journey President Young left his family no less than eleven times to return with his teams to assist in bringing up the poor and the helpless. He tarried a few weeks in Atlas, Pike County, Illinois; then moved to Quincy, where he efficiently continued his labors in furthering the removal from Missouri.

On the 18th of April he left Quincy for Far West to assist with a majority of the Twelve in fulfilling a prophecy given by the Prophet Joseph Smith, July 8, 1838, which was accomplished, notwithstanding the mob had said that that revelation should not be fulfilled, and returned to

Quincy on the 2nd of May, and on the 3rd visited Bros. Joseph and Hyrum Smith, his first interview with them after their escape from their enemies.

May 16th, he started for Commerce, since called Nauvoo, Hancock County, Illinois, and on the 23d, moved across the Mississippi river to Montrose, Iowa, opposite Nauvoo, and resided in a room in an old military barracks, where he labored assiduously, so far as his health would permit, to aid the Saints in making their new settlement at Nauvoo, until September 14th, when he started " without purse or scrip," on a mission to England, his health so poor that he was unable, without assistance, to go thirty rods to the river, leaving his wife ill and feeble, with a babe only ten days old, and all his children sick, unable to wait upon each other. After considerable hindrance by sickness on the way, and much teaching and preaching, he sailed from New York on the 9th of March, 1840, and arrived in Liverpool, England, April 6th. In Preston, on the 14th of April, at the first council held in a foreign land by a majority of the Quorum of the Twelve Apostles, he was unanimously chosen President of that Quorum. In May he took steps for selecting the hymns and publishing 3,000 Hymn Books, 5,000 copies of the Book of Mormon, and a periodical entitled " The Latter-day Saints Millennial Star." He organized the first company of emigrating Saints, numbering 41, who sailed from Liverpool, June 6th. His faithful and diligent labors in England in behalf of the Gospel were signally blest. In the short space of a year, between 7,000 and 8,000 persons were baptized into the Church, branches were organized in all the principal cities of the land, a permanent shipping agency was established and over a thousand souls emigrated. On the 21st of April, 1841, he sailed from the river Mersey, and on the 1st of July, arrived in Nauvoo, and was cordially welcomed by the Prophet Joseph Smith, by his family and the Saints.

In a revelation given to Joseph Smith, January 19th, 1841, occurs the following: "I give unto you my servant, Brigham Young, to be a president over the Twelve traveling council, which Twelve hold the keys to open up the authority of my kingdom upon the four corners of the earth, and after that to send my word to every creature."

July 10th; the Prophet Joseph requested the Twelve to take the burthen of the church in Nauvoo, and attend to selling its lands, to locating and advising the immigrating Saints, and to transact other business, which request President Young energetically complied with, also with his duties as a member of the city council, to which he was elected September 2nd, occupying the intervals of time in laboring for the support of himself and family, until July 7, 1843, when he started on a mission to the Eastern States preaching, gathering funds for aiding the building of the Temple and the Nauvoo House, and returned on the 22nd of October.

He continued his labors as before, was often in council with Joseph and the Twelve, preached frequently in Nauvoo and the neighboring settlements, and on the 21st of May again went on a mission to the East, received information of the assassination of the Prophets Joseph and Hyrum Smith, in Carthage Jail, while under the pledged protection of Thomas Ford, then Governor of Illinois, and returned to Nauvoo on the 6th of August. On the 8th, at a meeting of all the authorities of the Church in Nauvoo, the Twelve Apostles were sustained as the Presiding Quorum of the Church. It was on this occasion that the spirit of the departed Joseph rested down upon Brigham Young in so powerful a manner as to convince all the Saints assembled that he was the man chosen to lead Israel. It was a critical time. Efforts were being made to divide the people, and one of the late Prophet's counselors claimed authority to preside as "guardian of the Church." But when President Young stepped forth in his place and calling at the head of the Twelve, the whole assembly heard, as they thought, the voice, saw the form and felt the spirit and influence of the Prophet Joseph. And even non-members of the Church were startled, and expected to see the presence as well as hear the voice of the departed Seer. All uncertainty fled from that moment, and faith and union banished discord and defeated vain ambition.

Amid threats, houseburnings, plunderings, whippings, murders, and the fury of mob violence, he stood firm in the steady performance of the many and arduous duties devolved upon him, in caring for and defending the rights of the Saints, planning and directing the organizations and operations preparatory to vacating Nauvoo and forwarding the Temple to completion, and laboring therein until February, 1846, when he crossed the Mississippi River to the camp of the emigrating Saints, a few miles west of Montrose, Iowa, and in March began with them a toilsome journey in quest of a location beyond the pale of bigoted intolerance, where he would be free to worship God according to His commandments.

Having established two settlements, Garden Grove and Mount Pisgah, resting and recruiting points for such as could not well keep pace and for others who would follow, he reached, with the main camp, the Missouri River, near Council Bluffs, in July. From this point, at the request of the Government of the United States he sent 500 volunteers (the "Mormon Battalion") to aid in the war with Mexico, who raised and sustained the flag of the Union in Mexico and California until the treaty of Guadalupe-Hidalgo. He crossed the Missouri and camped a few miles above where Omaha has since been built, at a point named Winter Quarters, since called Florence, Nebraska, and laid out streets and blocks upon which numerous comfortable log houses were soon erected; planned to the utmost for the comfort and well-being of the people during their sojourn there; built a much-needed grist mill, and in April, 1847, with a company of 142 men, who elected him their leader, started to pioneer a location where the Saints could build and inhabit in peace, and on the 24th of July arrived where now stands Salt Lake City, and unfurled the "Stars and Stripes," on Mexican soil.

He at once took steps for surveying the beautiful city site, designated the blocks around which houses were to be built, joining each other, with portholes and gates until the people should be strong enough to build on the lots in safety; was busily engaged in directing and assisting in the daily labors and visiting neighboring localities; and, on the 26th of August, started on his return to Winter Quarters, where he arrived on the 31st of October, having met nearly 2,000 of the Saints on their way to Salt Lake City, where they arrived in good season.

December 5th, 1847, he was elected President of the Church by the unanimous vote of the Quorum of the Twelve, and also, on the 27th, by the unanimous vote of all the authorities and members assembled in a Conference held at Council Bluffs, Iowa, with Heber C. Kimball and Willard Richards as his Counselors. On the 26th of May, 1848, he started from Winter Quarters, with his family, for Salt Lake City, leaving his houses, mills and other property (this being the fifth time he had left home and property for the Gospel's sake) superintended that season's emigration of over 2,000, arrived in Salt Lake City, September 20th, and at once began to give counsel conducive to the general welfare. At a Conference held on the 8th of October, 1848, he was sustained President of the Church by unanimous vote.

A provisional government being requisite until Congress should otherwise provide, on the 12th of March, 1849, he was elected Governor of the then named State of Deseret, which continued until February 3, 1851, when he took the oath of office as Governor of the Territory of Utah, Commander-in-chief of the militia, and Superintendent of Indian Affairs, to which positions he had been appointed by President Millard Fillmore, and performed the duties of those offices with signal ability and integrity, until the arrival of his successor, Governor Alfred Cumming, in the spring of 1858.

During the thirty years past in which he has resided in Utah, he has labored indefatigably for the welfare of all who love truth, liberty and equal rights; has engaged in and encouraged agriculture, the erection of mills, and factories, the manufacture and importation of machinery and labor-saving implements, the opening of roads and the construction of bridges and public edifices; has pursued a conciliatory policy with the Indians, wisely deeming it not only cheaper but much more humane to feed than to fight them; has instituted the Perpetual Emigration Fund for gathering the poor, by which thousands upon thousands have been brought from poverty to the acquisition of pleasant homes and the comforts of life; has successfully completed a contract to grade over 100 miles of the Union Pacific Railroad, much of it the most difficult portion; was the prime mover in the construction of the Utah Central Railroad, also of the Utah Southern Railroad; has aided in building the Utah Northern and Utah Western narrow guage roads; has introduced and fostered co-operation in all branches of business, as the plan best adapted to equalize the benefits of trade; has extended telegraph wires to most of our principal towns and cities; has promoted the spread of the everlasting Gospel among the nations, and the gathering of the honest therefrom; has traveled and preached year after year in the settlements of the Saints; and in his teachings, acts and administrations has uniformly pursued a course characteristic of an able and upright man laboring with all his might for the happiness of mankind and the prevalence of righteousness upon the earth.

Like all great men, he has had bitter enemies. No man has been more villified, misrepresented and falsely accused than Brigham Young. His life has been frequently sought. The bullet and the knife of the assassin have been prepared to shed his heart's blood, and plots have been illegally laid by the emissaries of the law to rob, imprison, and destroy him. But the hand of the Lord has delivered him on every occasion, and the calmness and serenity with which he has invariably looked upon calumny and persecution, has stamped him as one of the largest minded men of the century.

He had a strong desire to live to dedicate a Temple to the Most High God in these mountains, set in order the Priesthood and organize the various Stakes of Zion according to the pattern revealed from heaven. These privileges were granted to him. He saw the Temple at St. George fully dedicated and prepared for the administration of the ordinances for the living and the dead. He arranged and explained the duties of the various quorums of the priesthood. And last Sunday the organization of the different Stakes of Zion was completed. His desire has been fulfilled, and now he has departed.

For some time past President Young had acutely suffered occasionally from ailments which assisted in weakening his system, but his strong vitality, powerful will and unswerving faith overcame the effects to a great extent. Last Thursday he was seized with an inclination to vomit. However, he attended to business as usual, and in the evening spoke at a priesthood meeting in the Council House with great force and energy. During the night and following day his malady increased and cholera morbus set in, supplemented by inflammation of the bowels on Saturday, to which disease he succumbed. He was attended through his sickness by Drs. Seymour B. Young, W. F. Anderson and the Benedict Brothers. The ordinance of the Church for the benefit of the sick was repeatedly administered to him. His family were summoned, as danger increased, and his last moments were cheered by their presence.

When asked concerning his own desires he replied he was in the hands of the Lord and was willing to live or die as He decreed.

Among President Young's last expressions were his thankfulness at being so well cared for and having his family near him to wait upon and administer to him. He said "You are all *so* good." The last words he uttered that were distinctly understood were, "Joseph, Joseph, Joseph, Joseph." Other remarks relating to Joseph were expressed, but in a manner that was not comprehended.

At four o'clock yesterday, he departed in peace to join the Prophet Joseph, to the continuation of whose work he devoted his life, and other noble servants of God who have lived and died for the truth.

President Young is the head of a numerous family, and has laid the foundation of a kingdom and a glory which will increase throughout eternity. He was the father of fifty-six children. He has left seventeen wives, sixteen sons, and twenty-eight daughters to follow in his footsteps and perpetuate his name and greatness in the earth. His family were devoted to him and he to them, and the deep affection of all for the husband and father, speaks louder than any words of praise in evidence of his kindness, goodness and paternal care.

We bid him farewell with sorrow too deep for words. But in the light of his teachings we look forward to a joyful meeting in the resurrection of the just, when the ties severed by the Destroyer shall be joined eternally by Him who has conquered Death, and holds the keys of life and immortality.

President Young has left instructions concerning the disposition of his remains which will be read at the funeral services next Sunday in the New Tabernacle at 12, noon, to which the Saints are generally invited.

Peace be to Brother Brigham, the large-souled leader, the wise counselor, the faithful friend of the good, the foe to evil, the inspired prophet, the great pioneer and colonizer, the loving husband and father, the indefatigable laborer for the salvation of the race! We sympathize with his bereaved family and condole with the whole Church. And may we who still remain emulate his virtues, profit by his teachings and live so that when we depart we may be worthy to mingle with the society in which he now moves, and to participate with him in the glories of that resurrection in which he will shine among the brightest and the best!

[From the Deseret Evening News, August 31, 1877.]

LAST MOMENTS OF PRESIDENT BRIGHAM YOUNG.

In order to satisfy the feelings of many of our readers and answer numerous inquiries concerning the particulars of the last sickness of our late beloved President, Brigham Young, we publish the following, arranged from reports made by Drs. Seymour B. Young and F. D. Benedict, and others who were present during the last hours of the President's earthly existence:

President Young's sickness commenced on Thursday, Aug. 23, continuing the whole of the afternoon. He had an inclination to vomit, but he continued to attend to his business as usual. In the evening he was present at a Bishops' meeting in the Council House, and instructed the brethren in their duties, speaking with marked point and power.

At 11 o'clock at night, on retiring, he was seized with an attack of cholera morbus, the usual symptoms of vomiting and purging being almost continuous until five o'clock on Friday morning, when, at his own request, a mild opiate was administered hypodermically into each foot, to relieve the intense pain, caused by the constant cramping of the muscles.

During the whole of that day his sufferings were great, continuing through most of the night, but becoming less severe towards Saturday morning, when he slept for a few hours. This was the first rest he enjoyed from the commencement of his attack. During the whole of this period he endured his pain cheerfully, and occasionally made humorous remarks as was his wont when he saw those around him inclined to be troubled.

Inflammation of the bowels set in on Saturday at 3 p.m. and the abdomen commenced to swell. One small dose, half a grain of opium, was administered, and at midnight the same quantity. These doses, though small, and given at long intervals, had a tendency to somewhat relieve the pain and retching, so susceptible was his system to any kind of narcotic or stimulant.

Throughout Sunday he continued, both while awake and asleep, to moan. When asked if he suffered pain his invariable reply was, " No, I don't know that I do." During the same night his sufferings were less severe, but continuous, although at eight o'clock he had a grain of opium and at midnight half a grain.

On Monday morning, at eight o'clock, he showed increasing symptoms of nervous prostration, by constant moving of the hands and twitching of the muscles of the arms. One grain of opium was administered, and from then till 12, noon, he suffered severely. Another grain of opium was given him and at 8:20 in the evening half a grain more.

About 9 o'clock he sank into a quiet sleep, resting without moaning. During Sunday and Monday he had received, at intervals of half an hour, a table spoonful of milk and brandy, an ounce of the latter to eight of the former. Hands were laid upon him by the various brethren very frequently from the time he was attacked until his demise. About 10 o'clock on Monday evening he sank into a semi-comatose condition, from which it was difficult to arouse him, although, by persuasion, he swallowed the milk mixture every half hour and a teaspoonful of ice water at intervals.

At one o'clock on Tuesday morning, warm stimulating injections were given, after which he thoroughly aroused, and, by the aid of his attendants got out of bed twice. At four o'clock the same morning he sank down in bed apparently lifeless. Artificial respiration was resorted to, by which the lungs were kept inflated, and hot poultices were placed over the heart, to stimulate its action. President John W. Young and others administered to him the ordinance for the sick, calling on the Almighty to restore him, and he subsequently revived, and responded "Amen" to the administration. For nine consecutive hours artificial respiration was continued. At that time he seemed greatly revived and spoke to those around him, saying he felt better and wished to rest.

This condition remained until about 8 in the evening, when partial prostration again ensued, and his case was considered exceedingly critical by the attendant physicians, Drs. S. B. Young, W. F. Anderson, J. M. Benedict and F. D. Benedict. After consultation an entire filling up of the lower part of the bowels by injection was determined upon, for the purpose of creating an action through the alimentary canal, but was not persevered in, on account of fainting symptoms, and the patient objecting to the treatment, which caused him to cry out with pain. He passed the night in a semi-comatose state.

On Wednesday morning symptoms of approaching dissolution were plainly evident. The early coma was entirely attributable, so the doctors say, to a poisoning of the blood, from a pressure of the swelled bowels, causing a prevention of return currents of the circulation to the heart and lungs. At the time of his demise he was entirely free from the influence of any opiates or narcotics, not having taken any for forty-eight hours previous.

From the time that President Young was taken ill until the hour of his death, Dr. Seymour B. Young attended upon him with the greatest assiduity, attention and care, scarcely ever having left his bedside during the whole of the time, night or day. In fact the same can be said of all his attendants, who remained by him constantly, and watched every pulsation and every change with the most intense anxiety and solicitude.

Dr. F. D. Benedict remained with the patient the whole of Tuesday night and Wednesday until his decease. Drs. W. F. Anderson and J. M.

Benedict also attended at intervals during that time. The temperature and pulsations were taken frequently, the temperature remaining at 99 until 4 a.m. on Wednesday when it rose to 101¾, and to 105 just previous to his decease. His pulse ranged from 120 to 128, the latter being reached after the administration of the stimulating medicines.

Not only the physicians named above, but the members of the profession of Salt Lake generally, expressed an anxiety to give all the aid in their power with a view to the relief and restoration of the President.

On Tuesday night about ten o'clock, while lying in a kind of stupor, his son John W. asked him, " Do you know me father ?" He responded, " I rather guess I do." About two hours previous to his decease, when several brethren administered to him, he responded in a clear and distinct voice, " Amen."

Since the news of the great man's departure have gone abroad, messages of condolence have been received from all parts of the Territory, as well as from different points in the Union and from Europe. No earthly potentate ever reigned more fully in the hearts of his people than did President Brigham Young. And throughout the Territory, while flags hang at half mast, and civic and religious organizations vie with each other in rendering tributes of respect to the departed, grief swells the souls of the Saints, and all Israel feels the magnitude of the loss sustained.

[From the Deseret Evening News, September 1st, 1877.]

LYING IN STATE—PREPARATIONS FOR THE FUNERAL.

THIS morning, about a quarter past 8 o'clock, the mortal remains of President Brigham Young were conveyed by bearers and followed by many of the male members of his family, several of the Twelve and others of the Priesthood, from the Lion House to the New Tabernacle, which is decorated and draped for the funeral services. The coffin containing the body was enclosed in a metallic covering, made for the purpose, with plate glass inserted of sufficient size to admit of a view of the departed. This was done for the purpose of preserving the sacred relics from the action of the atmosphere during the time of their lying in state. The whole was tastefully draped with white merino and wreathed with flowers, and after those present had taken a farewell look upon the countenance of our loved and venerated President, Prophet, and Brother, the gates were opened to admit the public. It was about half-past 10 o'clock before the anxious crowds awaiting admittance obtained ingress, the delay being unavoidable in consequence of the necessary arrangements above described.

It is the intention to keep the Tabernacle open all night and until 11 o'clock to-morrow morning, in order to allow those who wish, to take a last look at the face of him who has led and counseled them so faithfully for many years. A proper and efficient guard will be maintained in and around the building.

In consonance with the feelings of the hosts of Israel who lament the loss of one of the greatest men of the earth, the clouds, this morning, bowed thickly down from the skies, and throughout the day shed gentle, but copious tears, as if in sympathy with the multitude who thronged the entrance to the Tabernacle. Up to 3.45 o'clock, 6,000 persons had passed through the building to take a farewell view of the President.

A great number of people have come in to-day by team as well as by railroad. To-morrow, if the weather permits, the trains will bring in thousands, each road running specials at reduced rates to afford as great an opportunity as possible for distant friends to be present at the obsequies. And whatever the weather may be, the throng, no doubt, will be very great. It is hoped that all present will be as accommodating to each other as possible, that no one may be needlessly excluded from the Tabernacle or deprived of a seat.

President Brigham Young is endeared to the Saints, not only by his public administrations, instructions and counsels, his travels and visits in all seasons and weathers, continually, for their temporal and spiritual welfare, his liberal expenditure for every enterprise calculated to develop the Territory and its resources, and his general large-hearted, public-spirited course; but by private advice, correction and encouragement, showing deep wisdom and fatherly solicitude, on all kinds of subjects, simple and profound, touching the common affairs of life or involving the dearest interests of humanity. This he has done for many years, exhibiting a patience and a kindness as remarkable as his quickness of perception, tenacity of memory and ability to grasp and decide upon anything and everything presented.

To-morrow we will pay our last respects to his mortal remains, but the memory of his labors, and the influence of his teachings will never be obliterated from the minds of the thousands who venerate his name.

[From the Deseret Evening News, September 3rd, 1877.]

FUNERAL OF PRESIDENT BRIGHAM YOUNG.

YESTERDAY morning the glorious sun, shining bright and clear from a cloudless and lovely sky, ushered in one of the finest and calmest Sabbath days ever seen in Utah. Special trains from the north, the south, and the west, brought in vast crowds of people from points far and near to witness the obsequies of President Brigham Young. The pleasant rain of Saturday had settled the dust effectually, so that the great throngs which moved through the streets suffered no inconvenience thereby.

There was a continuous stream of living humanity passing through the Tabernacle until half-past eleven o'clock, to view the mortal remains of our departed President. By actual count, over 18,000 persons of all classes, ages, opinions and degrees visited the Tabernacle while the body was lying in state, manifesting the greatest decorum and respect. Several thousands were not counted, as they took their seats after viewing the remains without passing out by the recording officer. It is estimated that nearly 25,000 persons took their last farewell of the honored dead.

Before the services commenced, the metallic covering in which the coffin had been placed to preserve the body from the air, with its drapery, was removed, the lid was fastened down and the face of our beloved brother and revered leader was finally excluded from human view.

During the morning the following music was finely rendered at intervals, on the organ, played by Brother Joseph J. Daynes, and by the orchestra led by Brother George Careless:

"The Dead March in Saul."—Organ and Orchestra.

"Brigham Young's Funeral March," composed by Jos. J. Daynes —Organ.

"Wilson's Funeral March"—Organ.

"Mendelsohn's Funeral March"—Organ and Orchestra.

The seats in the unreserved parts of the Tabernacle were filled long before the time fixed for the services. The building was handsomely decorated. From the immense ceiling which arches over the whole interior without a pillar, strands of flowers were looped in rich profusion, a massive and elegant floral centre piece depending from the midst, while wreaths were festooned from column to column under the entire gallery, with basket bouquets pendant, and each column, with the organ, the stands and the whole front of the platform tastefully draped in black. The coffin, constructed according to the President's instructions, and decked with garlands of flowers, was mounted upon a plain catafalque, in view of the whole congregation, in front of the stands on which were placed elegant bouquets.

The President's stand was occupied by his Counselors—Presidents John W. Young and Daniel H. Wells. The Apostles, ten of whom were present, the Patriarch John Smith, several of the First Presidents of the Seventies, the Presidency of the Stake, the Presiding Bishop and his Counselors occupied their respective seats, as usual.

The south front of the platform was occupied by the Salt Lake City

Council, the Glee Club and the Band; west of them were the visiting. Presidents, their Counselors and the High Councils of different Stakes.

The north side of the platform was occupied by the Bishops and their Counselors of this and other Stakes. Between them and the stands were the phonographic reporters, representatives of the DESERET NEWS, *Salt Lake Herald, Ogden Junction, New York Times, New York Sun* and other papers east and west.

The numerous family of the deceased were in the seats immediately facing the stands, the President's four brothers in the front seat. The south centre seats east of the family, back to the centre aisle running north and south, were filled by the Seventies; and the north centre seats corresponding, by the High Priests. The side seats on the south, back to the aisle above-named, were appropriated to the Elders; and the side seats corresponding on the north, to the Lesser Priesthood.

The rest of the building was entirely filled, as were the aisles and doorways and every available standing place, by the general public. The congregation within the building numbered at least 15,000, while thousands of persons unable to obtain admission were in the grounds of the Tabernacle or in the streets outside. About 30,000, altogether, gathered to witness the proceedings.

Precisely at 12, noon, the immense congregation was called to order by Elder George Q. Cannon, who, at the request of the family, conducted the ceremonies.

The choir of 220 voices, led by Brother George Careless, Brother Joseph J. Daynes presiding at the organ, sang,

"Hark! from afar a funeral knell,"

to the tune of " Rest," composed by Brother Careless for President Geo. A. Smith's funeral, and only used on the two occasions.

PRAYER BY ELDER F. D. RICHARDS.

Our Father, who art in heaven, in the name of our Lord Jesus Christ we implore a measure of thy Holy Spirit to rest down upon this vast congregation, that we may worship before thee in the spirit of meekness, and the beauty of holiness, and in that right and proper frame of mind which belongs to Saints of the living God.

We thank thee, holy Father, that in thy kind providence and heavenly love, when the whole earth lay in sin and wickedness, thou didst break the darkness and send light and blessing to the human family by thy servant Joseph; that thou didst cause the angels of heaven to minister to him, by which thy will has been revealed again to man upon the earth, and thine authority has been restored that the righteous may minister, in the name of Jesus, the forgiveness of sins and the power of the

Everlasting Covenant by which mankind may be brought again unto thee. And we thank thee, Father, that after him, when he had sealed his testimony with his blood, shed by the hands of wicked assassins, when the church was young and feeble on the earth, thou didst give us thy servant Brigham to continue those labors, and to spread abroad the knowledge of thy will and to establish thy government in the earth.

O Lord, this morning, we are called to part with this, one of the noblest sons of thy numerous family; and we cannot but recollect the variety, the multitudinous character and magnitude of the labors he has performed here upon the earth. But we realize that we do not yet feel and know the extent of that loss which we have sustained by his departure. Thou, Father, hast made him to be a great captain in Israel, to lead thy people from scenes of deep distress to these retired vales of the earth, where homes, peace and plenty have been abundantly given unto us. Where he has been permitted by his labors and loving counsels to establish thy people in thy strength and blessing, by which thine enemies and the enemies of thy people, and they too in our very midst, have been vanquished by the power of faith that is planted in the bosoms of thy Saints. We thank thee for the great good he has been permitted to do on the earth and especially to thy people Israel. And we pray that thou will grant unto us that we may mourn for him in a proper and acceptable manner; that while we realize our loss is great, we may rejoice, our Father, in the anticipation of that joy which he experiences, with thy servants Joseph and Hyrum and those who have gone before of the sons of the father of the Faithful, even Abraham our ancestor. O Lord, wilt thou let that promised blessed influence of thy Holy Spirit, and the presence of their spirits attend upon us to-day, and be felt by this whole multitude; give unto us those sincere and intelligent joys of the gospel that shall lift our souls above every earthly care and sorrow, that we may be established in the principles of truth revealed and rejoice in the restoration of the keys, powers and authority of the gospel.

And we pray that thou wilt comfort the hearts of the bereaved family and household with such an exalted view of the character of thy dealings to thy people and to them, as shall enable each to say, "Father, thy will be done!" Bless the absent members of his family, his sons in other lands; may they in their ministry and studies feel the consolations of that Spirit which Heaven alone can give. Bless, we pray thee, the wives of thy servant who has departed. May they entertain that truthful, faithful and virtuous integrity to him which is most becoming for them, to share and rejoice with him in the fulness of the blessings of immortality and eternal lives. Bless thou and comfort and honor his sons and daughters, the commencement of a mighty race in the earth. O Lord, establish in them the powers of the everlasting priesthood and covenant, that they may be able to live to honor their illustrious father. Wilt thou remember his two sons whe have stepped forward and who are partakers of the apostleship. May they become great lights in their father's house, those upon whom the others may lean for assistance, for comfort and for support in all the walks of life. We pray that thou wilt comfort thine Elders in all the earth this day; when they hear of these sad tidings may the Holy Spirit minister to them, may angels visit them and make them to feel that all is well.

We pray thee to hasten the day when the great work in which thy servant Brigham has taken so active and prominent a part, shall be extended and magnified more abundantly in the earth. We thank thee, O Lord, that thou did'st inspire him in his later days to build and dedicate Temples unto thy name and to set in order the priesthood therein, together with all the ordinances thereof both for the living and for the dead, that thou did'st move upon him to more fully organize the people, set in order thy church, and clothe thy Zion more abundantly with the powers of the holy priesthood.

O Lord, now that thou hast taken him, let thy blessings come down in greater abundance and power upon thy servants who remain; and preserve thy people from any manner of schism or discord. And let those upon whom shall devolve the duty and responsibility of giving guidance to thy work upon the earth, abide in the bonds of the everlasting covenant, and may the revelations of thy will be given unto them, thy Spirit be in them, and thy counsels be made manifest through them unto all of thy people. And we forget not to seek thy blessings upon thy aged servants, now venerable in years, the brothers of thy servant Brigham. May they, our Father, be able to emulate most abundantly the worthy and glorious career of the honored dead whose remains are now before us. And we pray that thou wilt lengthen out their days until their souls shall be satisfied with this life, and then that they may be gathered to the glorious host that shall attend to wait upon them.

We beseech of thee, our Father, to remember thy scattered Israel in every part; the House of Judah, the Ten Tribes, wherever they may be, and the scattered remnants of this land in which we are permitted to dwell. May thy word go forth, thy spirit be diffused, and the power of the priesthood that thou hast restored rest not until Israel be gathered, Zion redeemed, Jerusalem built up and thy glory restored to earth.

We ask thee, holy Father, to receive our thanks this morning, for we acknowledge with gratitude the peace that thou hast blessed us with. Although thou did'st suffer thy servant to be imprisoned for the truth's sake, thou did'st preserve his life until he could lay it down in peace in his own house and habitation, in the midst of his loving family and devoted friends. Be pleased to continue peace upon our borders and in

B

our midst, preserve us from the horrors of war, for thou hast promised to fight the battles of thy people. While hundreds of thousands are falling by pestilence in other lands, here in our valleys, once a wild desert, but now the home of thy saints, abounds plenty both for man and for beast. For all this we thank thee and praise thee, O thou God of Hosts. Bless, O Lord, thy servants who may speak on this occasion. May their words be full of consolation and comfort to all those who mourn, for we all are mourners before thee this day. And may we who have been co-workers with thy servant, so live and so labor that we may come to a peaceful and happy end, and our last days be like his, that we may rejoice in our labors knowing that they are acceptably done. We dedicate ourselves, our families, this people and work unto thee, the Lord our God; it is thine, and we are thine. Direct all things to the glory of thy name, and unto Thee shall be all praise, glory and honor, through Jesus Christ, our Redeemer, Amen.

Choir sang

"Thou dost not weep to weep alone."

Tune "Bereavement," composed by Brother George Careless.

The following remarks were then made, reported, as well as the above and following prayers, phonographically, by Brother George F. Gibbs:

PRESIDENT D. H. WELLS

I arise with an aching heart, but cannot let pass this opportunity of paying at least a tribute of respect to our departed friend and brother, who has just stepped behind the vail. I can only say, Let the silent tear fall that it may give relief to the troubled heart; for we have lost our counselor, our friend, our President; a friend to God, a friend to His saints, a friend to the Church and a friend to humanity.

I have no desire or wish to multiply words, feeling that it is rather a time to mourn. Good bye, Brother Brigham, until the morning of the resurrection day, when thy spirit and body shall be re-united, and thou shalt inherit immortality, eternal lives and everlasting glory, and thy life-long companions who will soon follow after, will meet thee in peace and joy.

May God bless the Latter-day Saints, and may the consolations of the holy gospel, the hope of the glorious resurrection and redemption wrought out by our Lord and Savior Jesus Christ, pervade every heart to the consoling thereof, is my prayer in the name of Jesus. Amen.

ELDER WILFORD WOODRUFF.

We have lying before us the earthly tabernacle of President Brigham Young. His voice is hushed in death, and all Israel has to bow and submit to the mind and will of God. Israel will never again hear his voice until after the resurrection. I have no desire to occupy the time of this assembly, in eulogizing the life of President Young. His works and words are recorded in heaven, and they are recorded here on the earth; and that is sufficient. Let those of us who remain a few days study the counsels, the sermons and principles which have been revealed unto us through the mouth of this prophet of God. It will be but a few days until a great many of us who are in this assembly will follow him.

It seems as though Joseph was anxious to have with him, on the other side of the vail, almost all the men that labored with him and stood shoulder to shoulder with him in the flesh. I do not suppose there was ever a man breathed the breath of life who, in the short space of forty-five years, has done so much towards the establishment of the government and kingdom of God, as our beloved President. His life has been before many of you for several years, and to some from the commencement of his labors in this church. He felt the weight of this dispensation resting upon him; he certainly has been true and faithful unto death, and he is prepared to receive a crown of life.

About all I wish to do in my remarks is to exhort this great body of people who hold the holy priesthood, that during the few remaining days of our earthly life we continue, faithfully, the work that is now left us to do. "The Lord has given and the Lord has taken away, and blessed be the name of the Lord." The great desire of President Young in the last year of his life, as well as previously, was that before he passed away he might erect Temples to the name of the Lord, in that way and manner that men bearing the holy priesthood in the flesh could enter into those temples and perform their missions, for the redemption of the dead. This has been plainly manifested to all who have been much in his company. I rejoice that he lived long enough to enter into one Temple and attend to its dedication, and to commence the work of others. And I would say to this people, let us go to and finish these Temples, that we may continue the work required of us. I trust we will realize the importance of the great and serious responsibilities resting upon us who are engaged in the work which comprehends all others, it being the great and last dispensation of the fulness of times; that we, like our leader, may be diligent, day and night, in striving to carry out the counsels given to us.

I feel to thank God in my spirit that our beloved President has had the privilege, when his work was finished, of laying down his body in peace, at home, surrounded by his family and friends; instead of suffering martyrdom as did our former President, and as did nearly all the ancient Apostles. This to me is certainly very consoling, and I would repeat, Let us accomplish the work laid upon us by our beloved leader, so that when our time is ended, we can go hence and be welcomed into the society of Brigham, of Joseph, George A., Brother Kimball and the host of Elders who have dwelt in the flesh and proven faithful and true, feeling satisfied with our labors.

It is said that "blessings brighten as they take their flight." I have often felt in listening to the glorious principles of President Young, that the people here heard him so much that they hardly prized the beauty and the extent of the results and virtues of his teachings. Brethren let us give these things our serious attention and remember them and carry them out in our lives. Let us keep the commandments, striving in all earnestness to be true and faithful to the end of our work, so that we may share the joys of those men whose names brighten the pages of our history.

I would say to the bereaved family, may God comfort you and bless you and give you increasedly of his spirit. Your husband and father has gone to prepare the way for his family who must sooner or later follow after him. If you as his wives, his sons and daughters keep his sayings, you will be prepared to meet him in the morning of the resurrection, numbered among the faithful and worthy ones. And to my brethren and sisters who have heard his voice for these many years : Let us not forget the precious words of truth and wisdom he has taught us. We are living in a time of important changes. If ever a man could have been saved from dying through prayer, President Brigham Young could. But it was not in the power of man to keep him here. I believe Brother Geo. A. Smith was kept from dying through the prayers of his brethren and the saints, several months after he was called away. But when the Lord calls we must go. When we received word in St. George of the sickness of President Young, we stopped all business, and went into the Temple, remaining mostly for two days and nights engaged in supplicating Almighty God for his recovery, until the time of his death. Having finished his work he had to go ; and he is now beyond the power of pain and sorrow, sickness and death. He has been true and faithful to the end, and therefore all is well with him.

That God may bless us all, and help us all to realize the responsibility we are under to him, to our fellow-man and to each other, to the living and to the dead, is my prayer in the name of Jesus. Amen.

REMARKS BY ELDER ERASTUS SNOW.

I parted with President Brigham Young and a few brethren who were with him in Manti, Sanpete County, in July last; since which time I have been engaged attending meetings visiting and organizing the southern settlements; and was, at the time of his death, on a visit to our settlements in south-eastern Nevada. Through the blessings of God I have been enabled to return, in company with Elder Woodruff, who has just addressed us, in time to be present on this memorable occasion.

Shall I say it is a pleasure to have the privilege of meeting with the Saints of God on this occasion? It might seem paradoxical to use such an expression, but nevertheless it is true. The pleasure is not in parting with our honored, tried and beloved President; but it is in meeting with this vast body of Latter-day Saints and the thousands of Elders of Israel that are assembled on this occasion, who have come together to testify to one another, to the world of mankind, and to the heavens, the love, the esteem, the confidence and the enduring ties which bind him to us. We meet not merely to condole with the beloved family and relatives of the deceased; but we meet to condole with each other, and to publicly testify of the faith we have in Christ Jesus and in the work that we and our President are engaged in, in which he led the van, directing our energies and as the mouthpiece of God imparting words of wisdom, counsel and guidance unto this people.

I first became acquainted with Brother Brigham in the month of July, 1835. It has been my high privilege to be associated with him in the labors of the gospel from that time up to the present, to share the benefits of his counsels and labors, and to co-operate with him in this great work in which he has been engaged. It would be but a small thing to add my testimony, but which I know would be the testimony of thousands before me, as well as thousands who are not with us to-day, more especially of those who have been longest and most intimately acquainted with him; a testimony we are all able to bear, namely, the never-failing devotion of his heart to the building up of the kingdom of God, to the honoring of the holy priesthood he received, and to the carrying out of the counsels of the Lord and all things revealed through the Prophet Joseph, as well as all things which manifested themselves to him from day to day. pointing to the welfare of Israel; all the day long he has borne the burdens and responsibilities placed upon him, which he has honored and magnified to the end. I believe that all Israel will agree with Elder Woodruff in the expression, that if the anxiety and prayers of the Saints could have preserved him longer in our midst, he would not have passed away. But from the time I heard of his sickness, which was less than twenty-four hours before his death, I was not able to gather any testimony in my earnest prayers and supplications that he would tarry with us; but on the other hand, a deep seated feeling rested upon me that the Lord was about to call him behind the vail. And when the news of his death reached me, the first and most prominent feeling of my heart was, "Thank God that he has had the privilege of spending his last moments in quiet and peace in the midst of his friends and has gone beyond the reach of his enemies, who now have no power to annoy and persecute him." We are permitted too to mourn his loss in peace and quiet. Peace be upon Israel! Peace be upon his beloved family! Peace be upon all his beloved brethren and laborers in Zion and throughout the world! Peace be upon the multitudes of Israel who this day assemble throughout the land to testify their faith, their respect and their love for him, the congregations of the Saints who are at this hour in every part of the land in the act of worshipping, and mingling their feelings, their voices and testimony with ours for the same common purpose!

President Brigham Young needs no monument to perpetuate his name and character more than that which he himself by his own works and virtues has reared in the hearts of his people. And his testimony is such as will be in force to all the world, and his fame in connection with that of the Prophet Joseph Smith is known among all nations, kindreds, tongues and people. This latter-day work is not the work of a few years in mortality; our priesthood is everlasting, "without beginning of days or end of years," the labors of which reach forward through time into eternity and continue for ever. Truly did the Lord speak to John the the Revelator when banished for the Gospel's sake to the Isle of Patmos, "Blessed are the dead which die in the Lord, from henceforth: Yea, saith the Spirit, that they may rest from their labors; and their works do follow them." From the labors of the flesh they rest, but their works continue. Rest is a change, but not a cessation from labor. And the works of every faithful Elder of Israel after finishing his labors in the flesh, will go forward in the future ages of eternity. Brother Brigham, having done a great, a glorious work in the flesh, now joins his labors with those of the spirit world and is welcomed back again from this mission of mortality; receives the joyous welcome of the Father and the Son and the greetings of apostles and prophets, of Joseph and his brethren who have gone before him, all welcoming him back again from earth; he joins with them in the more extensive labors of the Priesthood, and the redemption of the hosts of the dead and their preparations for the resurrection day.

It is a great joy and comfort to know that he had the privilege of living to complete one Temple and to see it dedicated, and that he superintended the setting in order of the priesthood and the ordinances for the redemption of the dead, as well as for the exaltation of the living. It was one of the greatest objects of his life, something that he greatly desired to see done before he should pass away. I have often reflected upon the prayer that I used to hear offered up by Brother George A. Smith during his last winter which he spent with President Young in St. George. As Trustee-in-Trust he directed the labors of building the Temple. His frequent prayer was, in substance, that the Lord would spare President Young to see the completion of that Temple and to set in order the Priesthood therein. While I often heard him make this prayer,

I do not remember having heard him make the same request in his own behalf. Prest. Geo. A. Smith passed away without this privilege, but his prayer was answered on the head of his brother Brigham, and all the elders of Israel greatly rejoice because he obtained this privilege, for now all things pertaining to the ordinances and keys of the priesthood in all their minutiæ were set in order according to the revelations of God. And it will be remembered that after his return from St. George, last spring, on his first greeting his brethren from this stand, one of the most prominent sentiments expressed by him, when referring to his work during the winter, was that he felt satisfied with his labors; to which I believe all Israel so far as they were acquainted with the nature of and could appreciate those labors, could say Amen. He was moved upon to direct his brethren, the Apostles to go to and organize the Stakes of Zion throughout the Territory, in which he himself took a prominent part, according to the strength of body he possessed. And the kind, fatherly spirit that characterized his every act during this period of his life seemed to shine brighter and exert even a more peaceful influence than at any time of his life before. His public addresses, his private utterances, his counsels and labors during the past Summer, have all seemed to bespeak that the hour was drawing near, the time was close at hand when he should depart. I have watched him during the entire season while I was with him, and also during his late labors in the South in the Temple, and from that time to this I carefully observed every word that flowed from his lips both in public and private, everything tending to make this profound impression upon my feelings that he was soon to pass behind the vail; and on receiving word of his last sickness, the impression forced itself upon me, he is to depart. I can therefore say, we mourn not as the world mourn. Was he our leader? Yes, in one sense, and that only as we are in the habit of using that term. For thirty-three years, since the death of the Prophet Joseph, he has been our earthly head; and yet he was not our leader, except in the earthly sense; for the Lord wrought in him and through him and by him as our earthly leader.

And may God grant in his merciful kindness that he will never hide his face from us; but ever continue to lead us, as a people, to glory and victory, triumphing over evil, subduing our passions and repenting fully of all our sins, our selfishness and pride, our vanity and folly; and uniting our hearts as a band of brethren and sisters for the carrying out of the counsels of the Lord which we have so often received through him; and imitate his noble example, and practise those noble virtues in our lives. And teach them to our children and our children's children and spread them abroad throughout the world, devoting our lives and energies for the salvation and redemption of the living and the dead, until we too shall go hence and meet with Brother Brigham in the spirit world, to be welcomed back from this our earthly mission, receiving that welcome plaudit, " Well done good and faithful servant, enter in to the joy of thy Lord ;" and then when it shall please God our Father to cause the trump to sound for the resurrection, that we may greet each other again with the Lord Jesus Christ, and the apostles and saints who have gone before; which we ask in the name of Jesus Christ. Amen.

ELDER GEORGE Q. CANNON.

Nearly four years ago President Young, in company with a number of other Elders, wrote his instructions which he and they desired to have left on record concerning their funerals. It was his written request that his instructions upon this subject be read at his funeral. They are as follows :

I, Brigham Young, wish my funeral services to be conducted after the following manner:

When I breathe my last I wish my friends to put my body in as clean and wholesome state as can conveniently be done and preserve the same for one, two, three or four days, or as long as my body can be preserved in a good condition. I want my coffin made of plump 1¼ inch redwood boards not scrimped in length, but two inches longer than I would measure, and from two to three inches wider than is commonly made for a person of my breadth and size, and deep enough to place me on a little comfortable cotton bed with a good suitable pillow for size and quality; my body dressed in my Temple clothing and laid nicely into my coffin, and the coffin to have the appearance that if I wanted to turn a little to the right or to the left I should have plenty of room to do so; the lid can be made crowning.

At my interment I wish all of my family present that can be conveniently, and the male members wear no crape on their hats or their coats; the females to buy no black bonnets, nor black dresses, nor black veils; but if they have them, they are at liberty to wear them. The services may be permitted, as singing and a prayer offered, and if any of my friends wish to say a few words, and really desire, do so; and when they have closed their services, take my remains on a bier and repair to the little burying ground which I have reserved on my lot east of the White House on the hill, and in the southeast corner of this lot have a vault built of mason work large enough to receive my coffin, and that may be placed in a box if they choose, made of the same materials as the coffin—redwood. Then place flat rocks over the vault sufficiently large to cover it, that the earth may be placed over it—nice, fine, dry earth—to cover it until the walls of the little cemetery are reared, which will leave me in the southeast corner. This vault ought to be roofed over with some kind of a temporary roof. There let my earthly house or tabernacle rest in peace and have a good sleep until the morning of the first resurrection; no crying, nor mourning with any one that I have done my work faithfully and in good faith.

I wish this to be read at the funeral, providing, that if I should die anywhere in the Mountains, I desire the above directions respecting my place of burial to be observed; but if I should live to go back with the Church, to Jackson County, I wish to be buried there.

BRIGHAM YOUNG,
President of the Church of Jesus Christ of Latter-day Saints.

Sunday, November 9th, 1873.   Salt Lake City, Utah Territory.

If there ever is an occasion, brethren and sisters, when words are too feeble to express the emotions of the human heart, it is one like the present. This is a time of mourning, not a time of speaking. Still we would not be doing justice to our feelings, nor to the memory of our great leader, if we did not give some utterance to the feelings that oppress our hearts.

I have never in my life contemplated the death of President Young with the calmness that I have since it occurred; and I have wondered at myself. It is true it has been exceedingly difficult for me to control my feelings, to keep from breaking down; but there has been a calmness, a serenity, a peace connected with his death, his departure from our midst, that I think all have felt who have come in contact with him. His departure was like the falling asleep of a little infant. No tremor, no contortions; but as peaceful and as quiet, as still as if it were indeed the most gentle slumber. I have often heard President Young speak about death; and when I saw him depart I felt that the great wish of his heart had at last been granted unto him. Naturally he was a man of indomitable courage, of an unyielding will; and he could not submit even to the conqueror Death without struggling against him. This was characteristic of his nature. But his natural feelings, as I have often heard him remark, and I think he has expressed the same in public several times, were that he should hail the day of his release from his mortal existence as the happiest day of his life. Whenever it should be the good pleasure of our Father in heaven to call him hence, he would go, he said, with great pleasure and satisfaction. But as I have said, as long as life remained, as long as he felt it his duty to stay here, he would struggle, he would contend for life, he would not yield; but would endeavor to fulfill the mission which our Father in heaven assigned unto him.

It is only a few weeks ago, when conversing with one of the Twelve, I remarked that I would be afraid, if it were not for one thing, that President Young was not going to remain long with us. He was so hurried, was so urged in his feelings concerning the organization of the people; pressing matters forward, anxious to get the Priesthood organized and the Stakes everywhere set in order. He released all of the Twelve from presiding over local places: Brother C. C. Rich, Brother Brigham, junior, Brother Lorenzo Snow and Brother Franklin D. Richards, in the North; Brother Orson Hyde and Brother Erastus Snow in the South; all were released from presiding over the Stakes of Zion, and were told by the President that their mission had a larger field than a Stake of Zion. He set the Priesthood in order as it has never before been since the first organization of the Church upon the earth. He defined the duties of the Apostles, he defined the duties of the Seventies, he defined the duties of the High Priests, the duties of the Elders and those of the lesser Priesthood, with plainness and distinctness and power—the power of God—in a way that it is left on record in such unmistakable language that no one need err who has the spirit of God resting down upon him. And when contemplating the organization of the Church as it is, we can testify to the goodness of our God, and we can feel to accord to him all praise for giving unto us so great and so good and exalted a character as our beloved Brother Brigham whose remains now lie before us. His value has not been properly estimated by the Latter-day Saints. There are none of us who will not feel this more and more in the future. To-day, now that we have lost him, we can examine our conduct, and the wish will arise that we had been more obedient, more willing to observe his counsels and pay him that respect and reverence which his great qualities as a prophet and leader deserved. This we can do, even though we have been faithful and obedient. The time will come when the Latter-day Saints will appreciate him as one of the greatest prophets that ever lived. I have been much with him. I look upon this association as the greatest privilege of my life, to have heard his counsels and to witness his life as I have. And in contemplating that life, it seems to me perfect: In my eyes and to my feelings he was as perfect a man as could be in mortality. He certainly never uttered any counsel or gave any instruction or taught any doctrine which I did not endorse with all my heart. This I believe to be the case with thousands upon thousands of the Latter-day Saints, notwithstanding our laxity in doing the will of God in all things as we should have done.

On Tuesday night, as I sat at the head of his bed and thought of his death, if it should occur, I recoiled from the contemplation of the view. It seemed to me that he was indispensable. What could we do without him? He has been the brain, the eye, the ear, the mouth and hand for the entire people of the Church of Jesus Christ of Latter-day Saints. From the greatest details connected with the organization of this Church down to the smallest minutiæ connected with the work, he has left upon it the impress of his great mind. From the organization of the Church, and the construction of Temples; the building of Tabernacles; from the creation of a Provisional State government and a Territorial gevernment, down to the small matter of directing the shape of these seats upon which we sit this day; upon all these things, as well as upon all the settlements of the Territory, the impress of his genius is apparent. Nothing was too small for his mind; nothing was too large. His mind was of that character that it could grasp the greatest subjects, and yet it had the capacity to descend to the minutest details. This was evident in all his counsels and associations with the Saints; he had the power, that wonderful faculty which God gave him and with which he was inspired. And while I was thus thinking of all this, it seemed as though we could not spare him, he was indispensable to this great work. And while I felt it, it seemed as though a voice said, "I am God; this is my work; it is I who build it up and carry it forward; it is my business to guide my Saints." He is our Father and God; he is the Leader, he cannot die; he is beyond the shafts of the adversary. And he will guide and direct his people, if they will listen to his counsels, from this time forward, until they are led into his celestial kingdom.

And that we may remember our great earthly leader, and treasure up his teachings, his counsels, and instructions and that we may follow the glorious example he has set us in his devotion to the work, in his self-abnegation in putting away everything that would interfere with the fulfilment and perfect performance of his duties, as Latter-day Saints, is my prayer in the name of Jesus Christ. Amen.

ELDER JOHN TAYLOR.

To-day is a solemn day for Israel. We have before us the body of the man who has led us for the last thirty-three years. Thirty-three years ago I was with and witnessed the departure of our first President, Joseph Smith. He passed away under very different circumstances to those which have surrounded President Brigham Young in his last hours. Immured in prison, surrounded by enemies who sought his life, and attacked by a ruthless mob, savage and relentless, they took away his life, and he died by the hand and in the midst of vindictive and blood thirsty foes, who in the absence of legal offense, surcharged with deadly venomous hate, clamored for his blood.

President Young, after leading the Church, and buffeting the trials and persecutions to which the Church has ever been subjected, has at length, in these valleys of the mountains, after having accomplished the object of his life and done the work that has been represented here so truthfully by our brethren who have spoken, lain down to sleep in the midst of a loving and affectionate family and snrrounded by faithful and tried friends; with hosts of associations that were loving, sympathetic and interesting, who breathed nothing but condolence, kindness and blessings, and throughout the Territory the people as with one voice offered up their prayers to the Most High in behalf of their suffering, dying President.

Both of these presidents had the faith and confidence of the Saints of the Most High, and the guidance and direction of the Lord. And the feelings of the people as exhibited here, the gathering together of this Priesthood and the Saints which I see before me to-day, is evidence of the respect and kindness that beat in every heart and throb through every pulse; and it is gratifying to know that the same feelings prevail throughout the length and breadth of this Territory. As has been said, his name and his fame are known among all people, and a knowledge of these events has spread to the uttermost bounds of the everlasting hills.

All nations have heard of it, and all peoples are interested in these events that are now surrounding us. Not only us and them but the Gods in the eternal worlds. The former President, Joseph Smith, and this our late President, Brigham Young, meet again face to face in the eternal worlds. Both have triumphed, both have overcome.

As has been remarked, the work we are engaged in is not the work of man. Joseph Smith did not originate it, neither did Brigham Young, nor the Twelve nor any mortal man. It emanated from God, he is its author, his eye is over us, he is watching every movement and every transaction that transpires now, and that has transpired ever since the commencement, and will continue so to do; he will guide the ship to the latter end. It is he that has been our Grand Leader, these others now departed have been our brethren, appointed to lead and guide us, under His direction, in the paths of life. And although we mourn the loss of our departed friend, a brother and a president, and although the feelings of our hearts sympathize with his family and friends, yet at the same time there are principles greater and grander than any personal interest, or any individuality associated with these matters. It is a heavenly interest, the building up of Zion, the establishment of the Kingdom of God and the rolling forth of his purposes upon the earth. And while Brother Joseph and Brother Brigham sleep, yet both of them live, and both of them, as they operated in time, will operate in eternity in behalf of the whole of Israel and the consummation of our Father's purposes. These are things in which the Gods are interested; and all the priesthood, and apostles and prophets and men of God that have ever breathed, are also interested with us.

And it is for us, as Latter-day Saints, now to magnify our calling and our priesthood, honoring our God by performing faithfully and well the duties devolving upon us, that as the changing scenes we are anticipating shall come upon all nations—revolutions succeeding revolutions, we may have a steady onward movement, guided by the Lord; that we may progress and steady affairs among his people and provide a refuge for the distressed among the contending nations; that the light, intelligence and power of God may be in our midst, that Zion may arise and shine, and the glory of God rest upon her.

I do not wish to prolong the time; but felt like making a few remarks. To the family of President Young I say, "God bless you! The God of heaven comfort your hearts! May peace flow unto you, and may you be led in the paths of life, and imitate the example of your departed husband, father and friend! And you Latter-day Saints, follow in his footsteps, in the paths of righteousness. Let us obey all of God's laws, and all will be well with us. We are not alone! God is with us, and he will continue with us from this time henceforth and for ever. And while we mourn a good and great man dead, I see thousands of staunch and faithful ones around me and before me who are for Israel, for God and his kingdom ; men who are desirous to see his will done on earth, as angels do it in heaven.

That God may bless us all, and lead us in the paths of life, is my prayer in the name of Jesus. Amen.

The following funeral hymn, composed for the occasion, words by Brother Charles W. Penrose, music by Brother George Careless, was sung by the choir:

Death gathers up thick clouds of gloom
And wounds the soul with anguish deep.
Gaunt sorrow sits upon the tomb,
And round the grave dense shadows creep.

But Faith beams down from God's fair skies
And bids the clouds and shades begone.
We gaze with brightened, tear-dryed eyes
And lo! there stands The Holy One!

"The Resurection and the Life."
What hope and joy that title brings!
Death's but a myth with horrors rife,
And flees before the King of Kings.

Then shall we mourn and weep to day
Because our Chief has gone to rest?
He slumbers not in that cold clay,
He lives and moves among the blest.

We lose a leading Master Mind,
But spirit hosts behind the vail
New strength and added wisdom find,
To make our mutual work prevail:

Hosannas greet his entrance there,
And JOSEPH waits with words of praise,
While here sad thousands bow in prayer,
And funeral notes in grief we raise.

Farewell, dear brother Brigham Young.
God called thee through th' eternal gate.
Thy fame shall dwell on every tongue,
And Saints thy worth will emulate.

Thy work on earth was nobly done,
And peace smiles sweetly on thee now.
The crown celestial thou has won,
In splendor waits to deck thy brow.

Elder Cannon gave instructions in regard to the procession.

The benediction was pronounced, as follows, by

ELDER ORSON HYDE.

Our Father who art in heaven, in the name of thy Son Jesus Christ, we tender unto thee the gratitude of our hearts for the peaceful influence that has pervaded our hearts on the present occasion. We thank thee for this lovely day and the sun that shines so brightly over our heads, while the earth is illuminated with a grand display of thy glory.

We, our Father, in solemn assembly, have met to pay our last respects unto our departed friend and brother, President Brigham Young. We ask thee, O Lord our God, to seal the instructions upon our hearts and may the words which have fallen from the lips of thy servants on this occasion find place in the hearts of the honest and the upright, those who desire eternal life in thy kingdom.

Grant, Heavenly Father, to comfort the family of thy servant that has left us; may they find favor with thee; may the Spirit of the Lord breathe upon them, and bring them the balm of joy and comfort, opening wide the door for immortality and a glorious re-union with him in a time yet to come.

Bless, we pray, all the Saints here assembled; let thy good spirit rest upon all—that we may feel to renew our energies and that we may form renewed determinations to serve and honor the Lord our God, and to carry out the instructions we have heard this day, and not only on this occasion, but on former occasions, that we may become moulded and fashioned unto thine image and likeness; that when the time comes when we shall be called hence, we may be prepared and qualified to mingle our voices and join with those who have gone before us; where we can behold our leaders and join with them in songs of praise to God and the Lamb. We beseech thee, our Father, to let thy blessing rest down upon this attentive assembly, and upon the Priesthood here assembled. And while we contemplate that probably only one tenth of the people of this region are here assembled, we pray that our friends may be inspired with the spirit of intelligence to extend the same to all that are not present on this occasion.

O Lord, our God, bless thy people; confound everything opposed to them; and let the truth prevail, let Zion arise and let her light shine like the rising sun, that she may fill the whole earth.

We ask thee, our Father, to remember those also that have not yet joined the Saints of the Most High; remember them in kindness that they may be induced to abandon their hostility, and finally be brought into alliance with thy Church, that they too may ascribe honor and praise to God and the Lamb. And let thy blessing rest upon all. Forgive our sins; guide us by thy good spirit in the ways of life.

We are thankful, our Father, that thy servant who has gone before us is one that has fought a good fight, finished his course, and kept the faith. Help us all to do likewise, and thy name shall have the honor and glory, both now and forever. Amen.

The congregation then passed out, with the exception of those to take part in the procession. While the latter was forming the organ and orchestra performed "The Dead March," the choir singing, in harmony, "Unveil thy Bosom, Faithful Tomb."

THE PROCESSION.

Tenth Ward Band.

Glee Club.

Tabernacle Choir.

Press Reporters.

Salt Lake City Council.

President Young's Employes.

President Joseph Young, Bishop Phineas H. Young, Bishop Lorenzo D. Young and Elder Edward Young. (President Brigham Young's Brothers.)

THE BODY,

Borne by Clerks and Workmen of Deceased, with nine of the Twelve Apostles and the Presiding Bishop as Pall Bearers.

Immediately following the body, the Counselors of President Brigham Young.

The Family and Relatives.

Patriarch of the Church.

First Seven Presidents of the Seventies.

Presidency and High Council of Salt Lake Stake of Zion.

Visiting Presidents, their Counselors and the High Councils of Various Stakes of Zion.

Bishops and their Counselors.

High Priests.

Elders.

Lesser Priesthood.

Seventies.

The General Public.

Ropes, outside of which dense crowds formed, were stretched along the line of the procession to a point a little east of the Eagle Gate, and all the eminences in view of the route were filled with spectators, many of whom could not refrain from tears.

President Brigham Young's private cemetary is situated east of the White House and immediately north of Brother Le Grand Young's resi-

denee. It is in an unfinished condition, at present, but is surrounded
with a rock wall and so arranged that it may be terraced. It commands
a splendid view of the city and the valley south and west. In the southeast corner of this burial ground a stone vault had been made under the
personal superintendence of President John W. Young, and in strict ac-
cordance with his departed father's instructions, of cut stone, dowelled
and bolted with steel. Its dimensions are 7 feet 11 inches long, 4 feet
wide and 3 feet 3 inches high. It is laid in cement and the inside is ce-
mented and whitened.

Here the remains of our revered President were deposited, the vault
being surrounded by his wives, children, grandchildren, great-grandchil-
dren, his venerable brothers, his Counselors, all of the Twelve but two,
and a grand congregation of those holding the priesthood.

The Glee Club, led by Brother C. J. Thomas sang, very sweetly, " O
My Father, Thou that dwellest," to the tune of " Haydn's."

The following Dedicatory Prayer was offered by

ELDER WILFORD WOODRUFF.

O God, our Eternal Father, we present ourselves before thee, in the
name of Jesus Christ, to say that we have committed to this tomb the
tabernacle of thy servant President Brigham Young, and before closing
our labors and services and duties towards him, we wish to dedicate unto
thee this vault, with all its contents and surroundings. In the name of
the Lord Jesus Christ, and by authority of the holy |priesthood and
apostleship, we dedicate this ground and this vault with all the materials
of which it is composed, that it may be holy unto the Lord our God.
We dedicate this coffin, and the box which contains it, that it may be
holy unto the Lord our God. We also dedicate the body itself, the tabernacle of thy servant, unto the Lord our God, that it may be holy unto
thee. And we pray in the name of Jesus Christ that this body may sleep
here in peace a few days, until the time shall come when by the power of
God and the keys of the resurrection, it shall come forth clothed with
glory, immortality and eternal lives, with crowns, kingdoms, principalities
and powers, as they have been and will be appointed unto him. Yes, our
Father, this same tabernacle, which has borne the burden and heat of the
day, which has borne testimony through its life of the establishment of
the kingdom of God, preached the gospel of Christ and performed its
work faithfully, this mortal body which has suffered pain and sickness,
persecution and death, may it then arise in glory and power to attain to
its throne, clothed in glory and immortality, in connection with Abraham,
Isaac and Jacob and the prophets, and all the holy men who shall then
judge the inhabitants of the earth, even those who have lived in his day

and generation, to whom he has been faithful in bearing testimony of thy word and work.

All these things, our Father, we dedicate to thee and thy safe keeping in the name of Jesus Christ, and pray that we, with him, may be prepared in the morning of the first resurrection, and that we may be with him in the family organization that shall be organized in the celestial world, and that we may be prepared to receive those keys and blessings which have been promised through the priesthood and gospel of the Son of God. We dedicate all pertaining unto this place, this burial ground and all its surroundings, unto the Lord our God.

We thank thee, our Father, that thou hast revealed unto us that power and principle of the resurrection by which the pain, the sting and power of death are all taken away. For all these things, our Father, we praise thee; and pray that this dedication, in all its parts, may be acceptable in thy sight; and that these blessings may rest down upon the family, the wives, sons and daughters of thy servant Brigham, which mercies and favors we ask, dedicating all unto thee, in the name of Jesus Christ, our Redeemer. Amen.

The followers and thousands of spectators then passed by and viewed the coffin in its last resting place after the family had taken their final farewell and, "in a new tomb, hewn out of the rock, in which no man had lain," the body of one of the greatest men, and mightiest servants of the Lord who ever figured in the flesh was securely covered, to rest until the Christ whom he lived to serve shall call him from the dead.

Thus was concluded the grandest and most impressive funeral it was ever our lot to witness. There was a calmness, a serenity and a peaceful influence throughout the whole ceremonies which forbade confusion, and dispelled intense grief. In that vast congregation in the Tabernacle, scarcely a sound was heard but the speakers' voices or the notes of the singers and the instruments. Order was preserved until the close, and the two hundred special officers who acted in conjunction with the regular force, and who were courteous and gentlemanly, had no difficulty in maintaining that decorum which was a marked feature of the whole proceedings.

The President's wishes being fulfilled in regard to his remains, we have now to turn our attention to the carrying out of his inspired teachings in relation to the great latter-day work to which he devoted his life. Farewell, beloved President Brigham Young until the time when we shall meet thee behind the vail, or on the great and glad day when the Sun of Righteousness shall shed His glory on the resurrection morn, and thou shalt come forth in thy royal robes to reign eternally as a King and Priest unto God and the Lamb!

c

[From the Deseret Evening News, August 31, 1877.]

RESPECT AND CONDOLENCE.

In pursuance with a call by Mayor Little, a special meeting of the City Council was held last evening, to make fitting expression in relation to the decease of President Brigham Young, late member of that body. The Mayor, who presided, in his official capacity, feelingly announced the demise of the President, and explained the object of the meeting.

On motion, a committee, composed of Aldermen John Sharp and A. H. Raleigh and Councilors George Reynolds, D. O. Calder and John R. Winder, was appointed to draft and present appropriate resolutions.

Their report, which was received and adopted, was ordered spread upon the minutes of the Council. It was also ordered, on motion, that the preamble and resolution be published in the DESERET NEWS and *Salt Lake Herald*, and that a copy be engrossed and presented to the family of the deceased.

It was resolved, as a further manifestation of love and esteem for the departed, that the members of the Council attend the funeral, next Sunday, in a body.

Herewith we give the official copy of the

PREAMBLE AND RESOLUTION

Adopted by the City Council of Salt Lake City, at a special meeting held Thursday evening, August 30th, 1877—

Whereas, President Brigham Young, our most distinguished and illustrious fellow-citizen, and a member of this Council, in the providence of Almighty God has departed this life; and,

Whereas, The death of so eminent and so good a citizen, leader and member of our community, is a calamity so great that the mind seems inadequate to grasp, or language express, the extent of the loss that this lamentable event has brought so suddenly upon us; therefore,

Resolved, That while we mingle our tears and condole with each other in this sad bereavement, we tender this token of respect and love to the one we mourn, and express our deep sympathy with his family and friends in the overwhelming affliction which has befallen us all.

FERAMORZ LITTLE, Mayor.

JOHN T. CAINE, City Recorder.

TERRITORY OF UTAH, }
  Salt Lake City. } s. s.

This certifies that the foregoing is a true copy of "Preamble and Resolution" adopted by the City Council of Salt Lake City, at a special meeting held on the 30th day of August, A. D. 1877, as appears of record in my office.

As witness my hand and the corporate seal of Salt Lake City, this 31st day of August, A. D. 1877.

JOHN T. CAINE, City Recorder.

[From the Deseret Evening News, September 4th, 1877.]

RESOLUTIONS OF RESPECT TO THE LATE PRESI-DENT BRIGHAM YOUNG.

At a meeting of the Directors of the Deseret National Bank, Salt Lake City, September 4th, 1877, President Wm. H Hooper in the chair, the following was unanimously adopted:

We, the officers of the Deseret National Bank, realizing the loss sustained by this corporation and the community at large, in the death of our beloved associate and friend, President Brigham Young, who departed this life on the 29th day of August, 1877, in the seventy-seventh year of his age, hereby desire to express our deep sense of the great worth and superlative qualities of the revered deceased. Therefore,

Resolved, That in President Brigham Young we recognize a wise counselor, a financial genius, and a master mind.

That during the many years he has been a Director of this Institution, part of which time he was its President, having been associated with us from its inception, he has invariably exhibited such qualities of head and heart as have secured the respect, esteem and affection of all its officers.

That in his death we are deprived of a most valuable Director and adviser whose absence will be sadly missed from our official deliberations.

That we deeply sympathize with his bereaved family, and condole with the whole community, who mourn the departure of a mighty leader and one of the great spirits of our age and race.

That we bow in submission to the decrees of Providence, while we lament the sad event which has deprived us of so valuable a co-laborer.

That these Resolutions be spread upon the minutes of the Board, and that copies be furnished to the family of the deceased, and to the DESERET NEWS and *Salt Lake Herald* for publication.

By order of the Board of Directors.

W. H. HOOPER, President.